MILKED BY MY DAD'S MINOTAUR FRIEND

JADE SWALLOW

Copyright © 2024 by Jade Swallow

All rights reserved.

No part of this book may be reproduced in any form or by any electronic or mechanical means, including information storage and retrieval systems, without written permission from the author, except for the use of brief quotations in a book review.

CONTENTS

Content Warnings   v

1. Ruby   1
2. Stag   9
3. Ruby   17
4. Stag   35
5. Ruby   44
6. Stag   52

About the Author   63
Also by Jade Swallow   65

CONTENT WARNINGS

Please note that this is a work of erotica, not romance, with hucow elements that focuses on breeding and adult milking fantasies. This book contains an age gap relationship between a monster and a human and is intended for readers over 18.

Non-exhaustive list of content/triggers: An age gap relationship between a minotaur and human (20+ yrs.) Breeding kink (unprotected sex), pregnancy including fun times with a bump, dirty talk, lots of lactation kink (adult nursing fantasies), sex at the office, size difference, public sex, some pseudo scientific references (like hucow potion), some references to cow farming (sensitive topics for animal lovers), and typos and grammatical errors.

This is a work of fiction featuring imaginary scenarios. Do not try this at home. Only read if you are comfortable with the above themes. The author does not endorse the beliefs or actions of the characters.

If you read this book anywhere other than Amazon, you have an illegal pirated copy. I encourage you to research the effects of piracy on authors and obtain a legal copy instead. Thanks.

1

RUBY

I walk through the brightly lit hallways of Stag & Smith Dairy Co., my heart beating fast. With my college diploma in one hand and my new job offer in the other, I glance at the sterilized hallways of the building that overlooks a huge ranch. My phone pings with messages, and I nervously lift it up to read them.

Dad: Good luck! I'm sure Stag will take good care of you.

I sign, pocketing my phone. When I graduated, I didn't think I'd be interning for my dad's dairy company. Stag & Smith is owned by my dad and his minotaur business partner, Stag. They started it thirty years ago, and have since gone on to become the biggest producer of milk and dairy products in America. It's a multi-billion dollar enterprise, and I know I'm lucky to be handed the opportunity to work at such a prestigious company soon after graduation. Except, I don't think it's my dream.

I pass by the hallways filled with pictures of cows grazing in green pastures. The ranch with its greenery and fresh air makes me feel relaxed. My dad works at the city office while Stag works here, on the biggest dairy farm that the company owns. They have several across the country, and he often travels to check up on them. When I first found out I'd be working here, I was worried about how I'd survive at a ranch, but there's a supermarket nearby that stocks all the supplies, and the nearest town is just a twenty-five-minute drive. I get to live on the ranch as part of my employee benefits, which must be why they've managed to attract some good talent here. A lot of minotaurs and humans work at the ranch, though, I'm going to be working at the office. There's also a factor on the premises that processes the milk into various milk products.

At the end of the hallway, I spot a door with Stag's name written on it. Swallowing, I approach, knocking on the door tentatively.

"Come in." A deep voice calls out. I clutch the handle, pushing the door and making my way. Inside.

As soon as I enter the office with a huge desk and an open window, I notice the musky, masculine scent filling the air. My breath is knocked out of my lungs at the sight of a huge minotaur standing against the window, the morning light framing his imposing form. He's at least seven feet, with polished, white horns that tower over his head. Instantly, my belly pulses with need, reminding me why it was a bad idea to take up this job. Ever since I was in high school, I've had an unrequited crush on Stag. He's so much older than me, and a minotaur, but when I'm near him, all I can feel is the attraction searing my skin. With this back turned to me, he looked like an alpha, someone in charge. His legs end in powerful hooves, his back covered in a mix of brown fur and leathery brown skin. There's no missing the bulky, big muscles as his powerful, thick arms flex, making my pussy flutter in response. But nothing prepares me for when he turns around.

Milked by my Dad's Minotaur Friend 3

Stag's big, dark eyes lock with mine and I am gone. My pussy pulses, drops of moisture wetting my seam. The forbidden attraction between us turns the air thick with tension. I've never seen a beast as beautiful as this one. Stag is all muscle and brawn, and his powerfully crafted body is an asset in farming. But it is his face, that bovine snout, those big nostrils with a thick golden ring hanging between them, and those large brown eyes that are a mix of hardness and tenderness, that make my heart beat faster. My gaze trails over his bare chest, his erect nipples, and the leather pants covering his massive member that presses against the fabric, making me dream up dirty fantasies. My belly pulses, wanting this minotaur to breed me and put a baby in my belly.

"Ruby." My name sounds delicious on his lips. God, he's the Daddy Dom of my dreams, and I wish I could lay down on his desk and beg him to take me. After I went to college, I thought I'd be able to forget him, but none of the boys did it for me. Every time one of them kissed me, I found myself longing for this hot Minotaur Daddy and his mature, dominant charm. I knew those boys couldn't give me the protection and care I needed. No, only a man can do that. A minotaur, to be precise. "Your dad told me you were coming to work here. Congratulations on your graduation. John was really proud."

"Thanks." I flash a quick smile, trying to hide the flush in my cheeks. "I'm excited to start this job."

His hooves click on the hard floor as he takes two steps toward me, covering the distance between us effortlessly. I can feel his warm breath oozing out of his flared nostrils, his eyes taking me in. For a moment, I revel in the silence. I feel every flicker of heat and attraction that marks my connection to this man. Behind him, I see his brown tail move, reminding me how different we are. Yet, his masculine strength, his power, and his solidity attract me to him.

"I'm glad. We could always use more help. Things get hectic around the farm sometimes with the factory, the strategy office, and the ranch competing for my attention."

"I—I'll be glad to help you." My words come out low and sound suggestive, and I don't miss the way Stag's eyes darken. Could he...be attracted to me?

I've never considered that possibility before.

"You've grown into a beautiful woman, Ruby," he remarks, his voice thick. "Your dad is so proud of you."

I sigh, feeling conflicted at those words. I know my dad wants me to take over the company once he retires, but I don't think I want to do it. Since I was a girl, I've always wanted to be a full-time mom. My greatest dream was to have my own loving family and spend my time nurturing my husband and kids. After college, I'm even more determined to not end up taking over Dad's company. I know it's a huge responsibility, and I'm soon going to find the courage to tell him what I really want. Besides, my brother can take over. He's way more interested in business than I am.

"You're not happy about it?" Stag notices my discomfort, moving closer to me. I long for his touch, long to tell him that my real dream is to create a family with him. He's the man I've been crushing on for ages.

"I'm happy...it's just that...I feel all this is Dad's dream, not mine." It's so easy to talk to Stag, so easy to be honest with him.

"Is there something else you'd rather do?" His voice is kind and gentle.

Yes, marry you and have your babies.

"Yes," I admit. "Though I don't know how Dad will react

to it. He's always wanted me and Darren to take over the business. I guess I just got swept away by his convictions."

"If you don't want to work here, I can speak to him about it," Stag volunteers.

"No, I was excited to know I'd work with you. I need some time to think before I can face Dad."

Stag places his large paw on my arm. "I'm here for you anytime you need me." There's sincerity in those words, and I appreciate having a man who always has my back. He's kind and supportive and caring, not to mention he's extremely rich. Just the kind of husband every girl dreams of. Considering that, it's surprising he's never married.

"Thank you. For now, I want to focus on getting this job done." I flash a smile at him, feeling better now that Stag is on my side. I love Dad but he can be a little stubborn sometimes and having reinforcements always helps. I know he respects Stag a lot. They met three decades ago right here on this farm that Stag owned. After realizing their strengths were complementary, Dad and Stag decided to go into business together and created Stag & Smith Dairy Co. The rest is history.

"I want you to enjoy what you do," Stag tells me. "Though today's task might be a little monotonous. It's what our new recruits do on the first day."

"I've gotta start somewhere."

"I will give you a tour of the ranch and the factory, and then, I'll take you to the samples room. For today, you'll be sorting out some samples that we use to help the cows produce more milk. Our company's been working on an organic drug to increase our yields, and I think we've found one. The sample room is still a mess, though. I want you to discard the old samples and organize the new ones."

"I'm great at organizing things," I lie. "I'm sure it'll keep me busy all day."

"It's the best place to start learning about the company. Once that's done, you can start working with me in the office tomorrow. I'll be out visiting the cows at the ranch today if you need me."

Stag is a hands-on guy. While Dad is a salesman in a suit, Stag is an earthy, hard-working minotaur Daddy who doesn't mind getting dirty. He still has a sharp mind and an uncanny talent for knowing what the customers want, but his earthiness attracts me to him. Growing up in the city, I've only seen boys who'd scream at the sight of a cockroach. But Stag is at home in nature, one with the wilderness. That makes him so much more attractive.

"Great. I look forward to it."

~

Six hours later, I'm going cross-eyed from reading all the sample numbers in the sample room. It's like the cold storage of a chemical laboratory, filled with little glass bottles of liquid. There are endless shelves stacked with boxes of samples, some of the cow's milk, some ingredients that are mixed into the milk to produce various end-products like Cheese and yogurt, and then, there are three shelves full of the drugs, some injections, and supplements. A lot of them are outdated, and the farm doesn't use them anymore, which means it's my job to get rid of them.

I've gotten the samples spread out all over the bench and the floor, reading every number so that I know which ones to discard. Stag gave me a tour of the entire factory, and while I stood next to him, I fantasized about being there in a white wedding dress, saying yes to my minotaur Daddy.

Seeing him again has stirred up my feelings so bad. When I came here, I thought I could convince myself to go along with Dad's plans to take over the company, but after seeing Stag passionately explain every detail of the process, I think he should be the one running it.

With a dreamy sigh, I sit down, feeling something hard poke my ass.

"Ouch." I cry out, springing up, noticing that a syringe is stuck to my ass. It's gone right in, stabbing through my skin. I hit my hand against the shelf, falling back on my ass in that narrow space. As I do, the syringe is pushed, emptying the colorless sample into my blood.

"What the—" I feel the liquid go inside me, a strange heat filling my body. Hurriedly, I pluck the syringe off my butt, noticing how there's no more sample left. "Shit." I turn the syringe around and notice the number stuck to it.

HPS0003456788

I don't recognize this one. Hell, I don't recognize half of them. With a sigh, I put it back in the box of samples to discard, wondering why I placed this one separately. Since all these samples are meant for cows, I assume they won't do anything to my body. In any case, I'll visit the doctor tomorrow.

Yawning, I realize that it's almost five, time to go back home. I quickly finish throwing away the samples and place the ones I've sorted in the right slots. I'll have to come back to this one tomorrow, but my legs and back are aching from standing all day.

The door to the sample room opens and a familiar minotaur face greets me. "Are you done for today?" Stag's voice makes my tired body energized.

"Yeah. Just a few more to go."

"I'll help you," he says, squeezing into the narrow space

with me. His leathery hand brushes against my ass, and I moan. "Sorry, this place is quite narrow."

"It is," I admit, trying to focus on putting the samples back instead of my thudding heart.

"What're you doing after work?" Stag asks.

"Going back to my new house. I mean, there isn't much to do here. I picked up some stuff from the supermarket on my way. I guess I'll microwave some dinner."

"Would you like to come to my house?" He asks. My head snaps right, my eyes widening. Stag's big muscles flex and my mouth waters, noticing how big and brawny he is compared to my petite size. Now, I'm a classic blonde with blue eyes, and a lot of guys think that looks attractive, but when look at Stag, I can't figure out what he thinks of me.

"Since it's your first day here, I figured I'd cook you dinner. As a welcome gift." His voice is steady, so unlike mine. His presence affects me.

"I-I'd love that." Stag is a great cook. I've eaten his food many times growing up, and one of his hot, nourishing meals is exactly what I need after a tiring day like today.

"Great. Let's walk home together once we're done," he says. "What would you like to have for dinner?"

"Anything. Everything you make is good," I remark.

2

STAG

Soft, yellow lights glide over Ruby's smooth blonde hair, as she sits in my wooden mansion, gazing out at the starry night sky. Her perky tits are high in a tank top, her round ass clad in a pair of skinny jeans, she is temptation incarnate. The low lights skim her soft blonde hair, making me want to bury my nose in those silken and smell her shampoo. My dick hardens in my pants, and I'm glad she can't see beneath my waist, thanks to the kitchen counter.

My kitchen smells great, steam rising from the pot of cooking pasta. I'm making a cream sauce pasta using cream and cheese freshly produced on the farm, which is the fastest thing I can whip up. I know Ruby is hungry and tired after her first day at work, and I wanted to lift her spirits a little.

"Do you need help?" she asks, her striking blue eyes aimed at me. It's like a punch to my gut every time she looks at me. I swallow, trying to ignore the feelings rising up in my chest. I've always seen Ruby more as a kid, but after she went to college, something changed. She grew into a beautiful mature woman, and when I saw her again this morning, I knew there was no denying the attraction between us. Dressed in a pencil skirt that clung to her sexy ass, she looked heart-stompingly beautiful. Her blonde hair pulled back in a ponytail, her defiant nose pointing up, she is like a fairy who has stepped out of my dream.

"I'm almost done," I tell her, draining the pasta and adding it to my thick, rich sauce. It's cheesy and savory and with the truffles I'm going to grate on top, it'll have a nice umami flavor. Every time I travel to the city, I manage to get a bunch of ingredients. Not a lot is available here in terms of exotic stuff, but I've stockpiled a good selection of sauces and wines over the years. I toss the pasta in the pan as Ruby watches me, riveted, hoping the Tiramisu I made this morning is chilling nicely in the fridge. It was meant to be a surprise treat to celebrate Ruby's first day at work.

When John told me Ruby was coming over for her first-ever job, I was conflicted. I wanted to see her again, to experience the forbidden attraction of working with my business partner's daughter. But I also knew it was a bad idea. Ruby doesn't want to work here for long, and I wonder what her real dream is. My hooves noisily clutter around the kitchen, stomping on the wooden floor. Unlike Ruby who is small and elegant, I'm a big minotaur, a monster who takes up space. Everything in my house is large, from the lights to the big chairs and couch that dwarf Ruby.

She gets out of her chair, sniffing the air. "That smells delicious. I can't wait." Barefoot, she walks around my house, and my cock twitches. Her ass bounces as she rushes to my collection of vinyl records. I listen to them sometimes when I'm bored in the evenings. "You've got vinyl records. That's so classy." She begins leafing through them, and I

Milked by my Dad's Minotaur Friend 11

smile, glad to see her excited. She feels at home in a domestic environment, so much more relaxed than she was at the office.

"Would you like to listen to any of them?" I ask her, putting the final touches on the pasta. Keeping my apron on, I fish out the tiramisu from the refrigerator.

"Can I? Thanks. Your house is so beautiful and cozy. It must be a dream living here." She gazes at the wooden two-storied mansion with extra-large everything. The furniture is minimalistic, and I've got a few pieces of art and some exotic sculptures. It's a record of all the things I've collected over the years, some splurges and a lot of care. I'm proud of the home I've created, though it's a little too big for one person.

"It's too big for one person," I tell her, gazing up at the wooden staircase that leads to the second floor. "Gets lonely sometimes."

But having her moving around my space feels refreshing and right, somehow. I can imagine myself holding her next to me as we watch the sunrise and drink coffee in the mornings, cuddled up on the couch. The visual takes me by surprise. I've never considered getting married before. Since I started my business in my early twenties, it's been all about growing it. I've never really considered having a family, a woman by my side to experience life with, but as watch Ruby going through records, it grows on me.

I open one of my vintage wine bottles as she picks her favorite Whitney Houston record, smiling. "I think I'll go with this one. Mom loves listening to it." She shows me the bodyguard soundtrack.

"Great choice." I pour her a glass and walk to her to see her fumbling with the record player.

"Here, let me do it." Ruby's back collides against my

chest as she takes a step back. Worried she might fall, I put my arms around her, holding her in a back hug as she steadies herself. I'm so much bigger than her, my presence enough to drown her five-five frame. Yet, she feels so good in my arms, like she belongs there. "Are you okay?"

"Yeah. I didn't know you were behind me." I hand her the glass of wine, reluctantly letting her out of my arms. My big fingers reach for the gramophone and position it. In an instant, a booming power ballad echoes through my living room, making both of us smile. "Such a classic."

Ruby takes a sip of the wine and I keep my hands over her waist, swaying in rhythm with the music. It feels so wrong yet so right. Holding her in my arms, swaying like this is intoxicating. My cock gets harder, the fruity scent of her shampoo invading my nostrils. When I lean down, my protruding mouth brushes her soft hair. She sinks into my leathery skin, as my tail moves around her calf, brushing the exposed skin of her foot.

"Mmm...this feels so good. Unwinding like this after a day at work must be so nice." Ruby's words make me realize that what we're doing is inappropriate but she doesn't care. Instead, she takes another sip of wine before turning around. Her face collides with my chest, her small human arms going around my thick waist. Feeling her rub her cheek against my nipples and upper stomach is making me hotter. "Thanks for bringing me here. I've never been to your house before. Living in a ranch sounds like a dream." All I can see are her luscious lips moving, her face so close to my heart, making me question my decisions.

"It is a pretty good life," I admit, my voice tight, my fingers caressing her back. God, why does she have to feel so good? We need to stop or I might take things further and kiss her. "Dinner's ready."

I pull back first, and Ruby reluctantly lets go of my body. She follows me to the dinner table where I lay out her pasta, some more wine, and a salad for dinner. Taking a seat opposite her, we began to eat. Despite not lighting any candles or having any flowers, the moment feels incredibly romantic.

"Mmmm...it's so good. I missed your cooking at college. You know neither of my parents are good cooks." She eats spoonfuls of the pasta. "With the truffle, it's like eating at an expensive restaurant."

"I can cook for you whenever you want," I tell her, watching her delighted face. Taking care of her comes naturally to me. "Just text me and let me know."

"You're my boss now. I can't use you like that." She scarfs down the whole plate in seconds. Ruby must be really hungry.

"Well, I don't mind being used. Outside of work, you're not my employee." But I don't define what we are. I don't know what to call this attraction blooming between us.

"You're going to regret making that offer. Mom said I need to learn to cook. Maybe I should learn from you." Her gaze slides to the tiramisu. "Is that dessert?"

I hurriedly eat my pasta and nod. Either she's eating too fast or I'm spending too much time admiring her. "You wanna have some?"

"You're so nice to me." She smiles. I know Tiramisu is her favorite, especially the one made from Stag & Smith's mascarpone cream. I plate some up for her and hand it over with a spoon. Skipping dessert myself, I watch her eat it enthusiastically. She pushes her plate to me for seconds and gobbles it up eagerly. "This is perfection," she says, cream deposited over her lips. "I need this every day."

"I've got some you can take home."

"Mmm...I think I'm going to finish it all tonight." She

gets up, moving to the kitchen to get thirds. I go stand behind her, making sure she's all right.

"Slow down, there's some on your lips." When Ruby turns her face to me, my finger automatically reaches for the spot of cream on her lips, rubbing it away. But before I can pull my finger out of her reach, her tongue darts out, licking all the cream from my bare digits. My cock burns at the feel of her wet tongue flicking against my skin. It's unintentionally erotic, stroking a deep forbidden attraction I've been trying to deny for the last two hours.

"Ruby." My voice is hoarse, but when she looks up at me, her blue eyes are molten with lust. I can feel the tension in the air. Instead of letting my thick index finger go, she closes her lips around it, sucking it like she's sucking my dick.

That's it. I can't hold it in anymore. The monster in me rips out of my chest, pushing Ruby's small body against the kitchen counter. Before she can blink, I pull my hand away, replacing it with my mouth. My golden ring tugs against her skin as I kiss her for the first time. Her mouth is much smaller than mine, my protruding head eating up half her face. But the first hit of her lips is like an electric shock. My hands go around her body, pressing her close to me to feel my hardness as I rock into her hips. She moans into my mouth then I thrust my tongue between her lips, forcing her to open up and take my fat, thick tongue inside her delicious little mouth. I can taste the tiramisu, taste her unique favor coating me, coaxing me to abandon all self-control. My palm settles around her round ass cheeks, kneading and squeezing them as we kiss in my kitchen.

Our chemistry is blinding, making my blood pound harder. Ruby melts against me, putting her arms on my shoulder, and drinking me in hungrily. The air is charged with lust, every moment like the ticking of a time bomb. I don't want this kiss to end, don't want to stop feeling her warm body under me as I explore her mouth. When I pull my tongue back to take a breath, I can hear her moaning.

"Yes, Daddy...Don't stop..." Her forbidden words light my blood on fire. I want to be a Daddy dom for this woman, want to make her come on my tongue and all over my golden nose ring. I want to bury my swollen, hard cock inside her snug little pussy and fill her up with my cum. Dirty thoughts fill my head in a kaleidoscope of filthy scenes. Our kiss drags on, each hungry for the other. Ruby begins climbing me, putting her legs around my waist, and I hold her securely by the ass, resting her back on the counter for support. Her fingers trace my head, grabbing me by my gleaning horns for a more intense lip lock. Her taste is drowning me, making me forget that she's supposed to be my friend's daughter.

I need to stop. Now. But I can't bring myself to let go of her. When Ruby knocks over a glass, and it shatters, we come to our senses.

Using my last shred of self-control. I pull my tongue out of her mouth and stop kissing her. It takes all my strength to take a step away from Ruby, but the flush traveling from her face, right down her neck, and her tits is tempting me. I look away and before I can say something, I see Ruby move. She darts out from under me, running to the couch.

"Ruby, listen to me—"

"It was nice having dinner with you." Her words are quick and nervous. She picks up her bag and reaches for the door just as I catch up with her. "Thanks for the evening. I really need to go home now." With that, she opens the door, letting herself out and closing it in my face before I get the chance to say anything.

As I stand in my empty mansion, I realize that I royally fucked up.

3

RUBY

I wake up alone in my apartment, my body aching all over from last night's kiss.

Daddy...don't stop.

Embarrassment floods my face at the recollection of last night. I sit up in bed, noticing how bright it is outside the window. After the man of my dreams wined and dined with me and served me the most delicious meal of my life, he kissed me in his kitchen. My toes curled with joy when he put his mouth to me and ground that big erection against my stomach. It was proof that my love for him wasn't unrequited. I was so excited that I got carried away, climbing him like a tree and holding him so close. God, he's thirty years older than me, but none of that mattered when he kissed me like I was his last meal.

I can still feel his taste on my tongue, and every time I think of the way Stag French kissed me with that sexy, big minotaur mouth, I long to feel his tongue on my pussy. My nipples tingle and I feel like there's something wet on my breasts. I'm still wearing the tank top I wore last night, but my jeans are gone. I slept in my panties, replaying that kiss again and again until my mind gave out. When he removed his lips from me, I felt so awkward, and all I could do was run away like a coward.

Burying my face in my hands, I groan. "Great going, Ruby. Now he thinks you hate him."

I grab my phone, looking at the time. As I do, I feel an ache in my chest. Not the emotional kind, but the physical kind. I try to ignore it, focusing on the time instead.

It's already 10:10 in the morning, way past my reporting time. I totally oversleep. God, this is so embarrassing. I jump out of bed, deciding to take a day off since I'm already late. I don't think I can face Stag today, not after what I did last night.

I stumble into the bathroom, but the moment I switch on the lights, my eyes go wide.

"What the—"

My breasts are huge. That's the first thing I notice. Brushing my blonde hair back, I gaze down at the two melons strapped to my chest. I'm pretty sure I'm a B but my tits don't look like a B anymore. I blink, splashing water on my face to snap out of the dream. But it's not a dream. My new massive tits spill over the sink, my covered nipples rubbing against the sink's rim. Gargling mouthwash, I try to figure out what's wrong. How could my breasts have tripled in size overnight?

After brushing and washing my face, giving myself time to observe, I realize they're not shrinking. When I touch them, they feel tender and achy, like they're filled to bursting. My tank top stretches around my sore nipples, barely covering them. My boobs have gotten so big that they spill out the side of my top, jiggling like two big watermelons. They sag over my narrow waist, making my back hurt. Gently, I cup them, massaging them to ease the pain. As I do, the rough fabric abrades against my sensitive nipples, making me wince. My boobs are tight, and as I continue massaging, I notice something wet gather on my top. My nipples feel like they're surrounded by water. Did I splash water on them?

Impatiently, I peel my top off, determined to figure out what's wrong.

"Holy cow."

My massive milkers bounce free, solid, and real. Bringing my eyes to the bathroom mirror, I notice that my nipples have swollen to twice their size too. They're fat and slightly elongated, and the tips are extra-sensitive. But it isn't that bit that makes my jaw drop, it's the drops of milky white cream clinging to my teats.

What in the world is going on?

I place a finger on my white liquid smearing it on my nipples. As I do, more cream flows out of my breasts, more milky beads forming on the surface of my pink areolae. Horror strikes me. Is something wrong with my body? Why are my breasts leaking?

I swipe the white fluid, bringing some to my nose. It smells nutty and sweet like...milk.

Milk?

I lick the liquid off my finger, tasting its sweet, creamy taste.

It most certainly tastes like milk, but not cow milk. Human milk.

What if the fucking world—Am I....lactating?

The doorbell rings, making me pause my examination abruptly. I roll my eyes, wondering who it could be. After I was allotted an apartment on the company's property, they informed me that the property manager would swing by this morning to make sure everything was fine. I want to ignore the bell, but it rings again. Hurriedly, I wrap a robe around my new body, rushing to get to the door before I can think.

"Ruby." Stag's imposing frame fills the scene, his hot minotaur body making my milky nipples tingle. Somehow, my horniness has been intensified, thanks to the milk. His dark gaze rakes my body, pausing on my inflated tits for a moment before meeting my eyes. "We need to talk."

He pushes in and I get out of his way, hearing my apartment door close behind me. Since the rest of the employees are at work, I'm the only one in the complex at this time. Stag's huge presence fills my space, making me feel tiny in comparison.

"You didn't come to work today," he says. "Does that have something to do with last night's kiss?" Before I can say anything, he puts his head in his palm, smoothing it over his tired eyes. It looks like he didn't sleep last night. "I'm sorry. I shouldn't have kissed you like that. It's just that...I couldn't stop myself. You were there before me and I...something came over me. If it made you uncomfortable—"

"No, it's not about that," I tell him. My eyes meet his, and I swallow. "I...enjoyed the kiss."

His big cow eyes widen. "You did? But you ran out as soon as it was over."

"Because...well....I was embarrassed." Maybe it's time to tell him how I feel about him. With him in my apartment, asking me questions, it's going to be hard to deny my feelings.

"Why?"

Because I've had a crush on you since I turned sixteen.

My breasts ache and I emit a sultry moan. Stag notices.

"What is wrong? Are you sick?" He moves closer to me, scanning my body for any abnormalities. There are two of them stuck to my chest.

"Ummm...something like that." God, this is so mortifying. I kissed him last night, and now, I'm producing milk? Stag will think I'm such a scatterbrain.

"Do you want to tell me what's wrong? I could call the doctor—"

"No!" I don't want to show the doctor my new lactating breasts, even though I know that's what I should do. I need some time to get used to this development. Maybe they'll disappear on their own. "I...I just need some rest."

"I'm sorry to drop by unannounced," Stag says. "I was worried about you after you ran away yesterday. It was wrong of me to have kissed you like that...You're my business partner's daughter. I'm old enough to be your father."

"I don't care about your age," I tell him. "I've liked you since I was sixteen."

"What? Really?" It's his turn to be surprised now. My face colors, realizing I just spat out my greatest secret. "I...didn't know."

"You know now." My heart is in my throat. I just confessed to him, and I have no idea how he's going to respond. It's too early in the morning to be taking risks on my heart. "Last night...I really wanted you. I begged you to kiss me, remember?"

Daddy...

The forbidden words echo in my skull. I called him Daddy and I want to do it again. My body responds to my arousal, and before I know it, Stag is staring at my chest. I glance down and notice that my robe is wet. Two coin-sized spots of cream are spreading over the fabric, giving away my secret.

"Oh my god!" I jump back, startled. As I do, my tits bounce, leaking even more cream. "I can't believe this is happening."

"What's wrong, Ruby?" Stag steps forward and I lose balance, stumbling backward. He catches me, but as I fall into his arms, my robe loosens, revealing half of my creamy breasts. Stag's eyes go wide, noticing how big my boobs are. Milk streams from the side, forming white streaks all over. They gather in my cleavage, exposing my embarrassing secret.

"Is that...milk?" Stag leans over, his big cow tongue exploding from his mouth to lick the liquid covering my breasts. The flick of his thick, wet tongue on my sensitive skin makes my pussy drip in response. As he licks my milk cream, forbidden, dirty thoughts take over my mind, my core burning. His cool, metal nose ring rubs against my soft skin, making me want to beg him to put his mouth on my aching tips and suckle my milk. He lifts his eyes, swallowing the milk. "You're...lactating."

A blush covers my face. I thought Stag would be grossed out when he found out that my body was producing milk, but the way he licked my breasts like a hungry monster made me realize he might be turned on instead. My body heats another degree at the thought of this hot minotaur Daddy milking me and burying his thick cock in my pulsing pussy. It's what I've been dreaming of since last night.

"Yeah, I think I am. There's something wrong with my breasts." Saying those words out loud makes my face go tomato red. I can't believe I just talked about my breasts to the man who kissed me last night. "I was fine yesterday but when I woke up this morning... my boobs were hurting. I went into the bathroom and...found this." I gaze at my new, impressive rack. "I have no idea what could've caused this."

"I do." Stag puts his nose next to my wet patch and sniffs. His eyes snap up to me. "Are you pregnant?"

"What? No!" The words immediately burst out of my

mouth. After my disappointments in the first two years of college, I stopped sleeping around with boys. I've been single for a while. "That's not possible."

"Then..." As Stag's hot breath falls on my semi-exposed tits, my mind reels back to the incident at the sample room last night. "That sample...oh my god, could it have been that?"

"Sample?"

"I accidentally stabbed myself with a syringe yesterday while I was organizing the samples. It contained something, but I'm not sure what it was. I thought it wouldn't work on me since it was for cows but..."

"Why didn't you tell me about that yesterday?" he asks. "Some of those samples can be dangerous." I swallow. "Do you know which one it was?"

"I took a picture of it." Thankfully, I took a picture of the numbers while I was sorting them out earlier. Stag legs me go and I stand up, adjusting my robe. I hurry to my phone and bring it to him, and his eyes widen as he takes in the number and sighs.

"It's better than I thought."

"You recognize it?"

"Yeah, one of our scientists brought in a lot of samples before he devised our new organic medicine for the cows. This one's a hormone that's used to make human women lactate."

"What!?" My shriek resounds in the room.

"That's the reason your body is producing milk," he says. "We should go see a doctor. He'll be able to prescribe something to make it go away."

"I can't go there like this. I'll be leaking all over the place."

"I could go into town and get you a breast pump. I think

that's what mothers use. It'd take me at least three hours, though."

"I'm already full to bursting," I tell him. "If I don't get relief soon, I think I'll go crazy."

"Then, there's only one thing left to do." Stag's face is determined, his horns locked in position as he looks at me. "Let me milk you."

The moment those words leave his mouth, my pussy flips over with joy. My throat goes dry, and I can't stop licking my lips. Did Stag just say he'd...milk me?

"Babygirl, you've gotta make up your mind." His deep voice makes flickers spark in my belly. Hearing him call me babygirl is just too much for my brain to take. "You said you liked me, and I want to tell you that I like you too. In fact, ever since you stepped on this ranch, I've been crazy about you. After last night, I don't know if I can stay away."

His voice is guttural and his dirty confession makes my heartbeat rise. "Really? You're attracted to me?"

"I'm extremely attracted to you," he says. "I'd bend you over that couch and fuck you right now if I had my way. I'm dying to touch those milky tits, to put my mouth to your aching buds and feast on your sweet cream." My pussy is leaking steadily, aroused by his dirty words. "But I want you to decide. If we start this, there will be no stopping me." I can sense his desire for me, and I love that he craves me. I can't believe this is really happening.

My aching breasts make the final decision. I need him so bad. Inhaling, I undo the sash of my robe and slip it off my shoulders. As it slithers to the ground, Stag's jaw drops at the sight of my bared, milky breasts. Streams of cream cover my flat stomach and my heavy mounds, sliding right between my legs. I'm not wearing anything except my panties, and he knows it.

I take a step forward, sensing how hard Stag's cock goes at the sight of my milky body. When we're two inches apart, I say, "Milk me, Daddy."

~

STAG IS onto me in seconds, lifting my body off the floor like I weigh less than a feather. "Which one is the bedroom?" he asks, and I point to the only door in the apartment. He kicks it open, and then, we're in my bedroom. It has a queen-sized bed, assuming it's for couples, but it's still too small for my minotaur Daddy. Stag lays me down on the bed and climbs over me.

I hear the ripping of fabric and then, his pants are gone. My jaw drops as I glimpse my bid Daddy's cock for the first time. It's huge and ruddy, his massive, girthy shaft throbbing. There are veins all over it, but the size is definitely bigger than anything I've ever seen. He's a monster, indeed. Two fat balls dangle behind a patch of brown hair, and I swallow when I realize they're filled with his baby-making seed. My womb cramps, aching to feel him fill me with his hot cum.

"You're huge," I comment, as Stag approaches me, his hooves steady. "Are you for real?"

He laughs. "I'm a monster, Ruby. We're built differently than humans."

"I can see that." I smile. My aroused tits leak milk and Stag's eyes go to my aching breasts. "Is that thing even going to fit inside me?"

"We'll make it fit, baby." The bed slumps when Stag climbs atop me, his dark eyes gazing into mine. His meaty shaft throbs against my thigh, making my pussy leak cream steadily. "When we're in bed, you're to call me Daddy. Understood?"

"Yes, Daddy." The words are filthy and forbidden, but it's just what I want. I've longed for this moment for years. Stag's heavy body covers mine as his thick, cow tongue slips out to lick my fat boobies. The tip of his tongue circles my puffy areolae, sampling my milk before he swipes it all over my fat breasts. The cool air brushes my wet tits, making my nipples hard and aroused. "Mmm...you taste so sweet, Ruby. Your milk is thicker than the cows'. Daddy loves your beautiful hucow tits," he says, cupping my milky breasts with his hands. They're massive and I love how good they feel, milking me like a cow. He gently massages my fat udders, squeezing them from root to tip to get the milk flowing. When a jet of white cream streams out, his mouth closes around one fat tip and suckles.

"Ohhh..." Pleasure and relief spiral through my core as my letdown hits. His protruding mouth fits against my pillowy breasts, guzzling milk from my titty like a hungry calf. With every suckle, he makes my arousal flare, until I'm desperately rubbing my thighs together, aching for his monster cock. Milk flows out of my engorged breasts into his mouth, nourishing him with my cream. As a minotaur, he loves milk, and I feel glad to be able to feed him straight from the source. Stag's muscular body leans against me, his hard muscles pinning me down. His arms are thick and powerful like tree stumps, and I cling to him, surrendering my body to this alpha. Being milked by my dad's minotaur friend is the culmination of all my fantasies.

"Yes, my little hucow," he moans against my flesh. "Stay still and drip for your Daddy just like that. I love drinking your sweet cream."

Stag's hand finds my unused nipple and plays with it,

rolling it around between his fingers. He palms my breast, relieving my ache slightly with his hands. Meanwhile, he stops kneading the breast that he's feasting on, sliding down my flat stomach to the aching spot between my legs. Using one thick digit, he teases my wet slit, making goosebumps break all over my skin. I love how he takes care of my body thoroughly. He intuitively knows where I'm aching, and where I need him. When he rubs my clit, I arch my back in pleasure, moaning and thrusting my tit deeper into his mouth. I push my squishy nipple further in, loving how he sucks half my breast in. His blunt teeth graze against my wet, sensitive teats, making my core grow hotter. Meanwhile, he uses two fingers to pinch my clit and roll it around playfully. Pleasure shoots through my body, making sparks flare up all over my skin.

I grab the bull by the horns, enjoying our dirty milking session. Every suckle and tug on my teats makes my pussy wetter, making me long to swallow that massive cock between my legs.

When he releases my nipple with a plop, I sigh. One breast drained, and his greedy eyes turn to the other, palming it in preparation for milking. Who knew being milked by a minotaur would feel so good?

"Are you doing all right, babygirl?" he asks, still playing with my clit.

"Yes..." I can't form words. I need his mouth on my breast and his fingers in my pussy. My brain is melting under all that sexiness. Stag stops playing with my clit and begins circling my wet cunt with his finger.

"I think your pussy's getting a little lonely, darling." He thrusts his finger in and I cry out. Milk bubbles out of my engorged mound and Stag puts his mouth to my tip to suckle my cream. His finger is thick and leathery, filling up my pussy like a cock. My body turns to liquid as he pushes another finger in, giving me a good stretch before curving his fingers inside me to brush my sweet spot. A current of rapture hits my brain, taking me to paradise for one second.

"Do it again..." I whine. "Play with my pussy, Daddy."

"Does my babygirl like it when I touch her sweet spot?" He teases, suckling another mouthful of milk while his fingers rub my G-spot again. How this man knows all my exogenous zones so well is beyond me. He plays my body like a violin, every touch leaving an indelible mark on me. I guess that's the benefit of being with an experienced minotaur like him. He's the perfect Daddy Dom—sweet, tender, caring, yet hot as hell.

My wet pussy walls clench around his fingers, needing more. The way his mouth tugs on my teat, teasing and sucking on it makes a deep need balloon in my core. I can feel his cock swollen and throbbing against my thigh, dripping pre-cum all over my skin, and a need makes my pussy clench.

"Damn, baby, you're milking Daddy's fingers. Is my babygirl hungry for cock?" He reads my mind, licking my nipple between sucks. I love how he keeps me aroused, his fingers plugging my pussy and his mouth teasing my milky tits.

"Yes...Daddy, please..." I cry out, all the blood in my body rushing between my legs. My pussy is a hungry anaconda and she wants to eat my minotaur Daddy's monster cock alive.

Stag retracts his fingers from between my legs, and soon, it's replaced with his cock. My Daddy positions the head of his monstrous erection at the opening of my cunt and pushes in.

"Ohhhh...." Heat blazes through my core as his fat dick

pushes inside my dainty channel. I feel the stretch even before he's halfway in, his giant dick skewering my pussy in half. My inner muscles pulse, welcoming my Daddy's dick in.

"You're doing so good, baby. Let Daddy in...just a little more." Stag presses encouraging wet kisses all over my face, his massive hips pounding into my tiny snatch. My pussy stretches to the max, hungrily sucking my Daddy's inhuman girth. It's too big for me, but the stretch is so delicious, and even though it burns, I know it's going to feel good later. I cry and bury my nails in his leathery brown skin, pulling at the bits of fur next to his neck as I close my eyes and let Stag claim me completely. He suckles from my tits, keeping me aroused and wet until he's finally seated deep inside my pussy. "You did good, Ruby. Open your eyes."

I open my eyes and I can see his massive cock plugging up my pussy, his fat balls dangling against my ass. I rub my stomach and feel his dick inside me, that's how big it is. "Woah. I don't think my body was built to take a monster cock."

"On the contrary," Stag rumbles in a low voice. "Your body was only made to take a monster's cock. Only Daddy's cock can make you feel good, baby. Look how that greedy pussy is grabbing and choking me like she wants to milk my cum. Are you that horny, babygirl?"

He's right, of course. It feels so foreign to have him inside me, yet, I want him to stay there. "Yes, Daddy. I've wanted you for so long. I can't believe you're inside me now. I never want this moment to end."

He laughs, the vibrations rumbling in his chest and melting against my fingers. "I'm gonna start moving, babygirl, or I'll choke to death inside you." His hips rock against mine in slow, gentle, shallow thrusts, warming me up. It feels so good when he ruts into my pussy, that massive cock making my entire body rock. My fat tits jiggle, slapping Stag's face. He pushes me down with his hands, keeping my hips steady before grabbing both my fat, drained tits and swallowing both nipples together. My pussy twitches violently along his length as my sore nipples kiss inside his mouth, being suckled by the most expert tongue. Stag's thrusts get deeper as he pulls and suckles my nipples together.

"Oh my god, Daddy..." I am a little calf being taken along for the ride by the biggest bull on the farm. I grab his horns, trying to stay on the bed as he drills my pussy with his humongous erection. Stag pulls out and slams back into my hot little oven, making me see light spots. My muscles clench everywhere, my cells bursting with life. "Stag..."

His cock scrapes my insides as he fucks me ruthlessly on the bed, kissing and licking my fat titties. I love the way his pulsing, veiny length moves in and out of my wet, pink pussy, filling me up again and again, rubbing against my G-spot, and making my orgasm flare out of control. I was born to be dominated and fucked by this minotaur Daddy, and every cell in my body knows it. My pussy clenches violently around his cock when he scrapes the opening of my womb, begging him to deposit his seed inside my empty chamber.

"Does my babygirl want to be bred?" he asks in that low, dirty voice. "Is your pussy dying to be filled with my cum?"

Every dirty word is music to my ears.

"Yes, Daddy," I reply, offering no resistance. I know we're both swept up in a heated fantasy, but I mean every word. I want him to give me his babies, and make my belly swell with his seed. My heart swells at the thought of carrying his child, and I know instinctively that he'd be the perfect dad.

"Then, come for me, baby. Show me what a good girl

Milked by my Dad's Minotaur Friend 31

you are." His final, forceful thrust makes my body erupt into a shattering climax. Bliss washes over my senses, drowning me in joy. My screams are loud enough to shatter glass, but I can't stop. Clinging to Stag's horns, loving how his mouth tickles my breasts, I come around his cock, drenching him with my honey. My pussy convulses, my walls milking my big Daddy's dick for that baby-making seed. He rides me like a bull, prolonging my pleasure and taking me even higher.

"Damn, honey, you're making me come too." His fingers dig into my hips. He's so big that he can break me in two, yet I can feel myself getting stronger, needing this big monster more than ever.

"Come inside, me, Daddy."

I feel it when Stag climaxes. His cock swells in my channel and explodes, pumping my empty pussy full of cum. I close my eyes and feel each delicious rope of thick, hot fluid lash against my insides, giving me the most delicious orgasm of my life. Stag's fat balls steadily spew seed into my empty womb, breeding me as we come together, our fingers locked, our sweaty-naked bodies rubbing together. His leathery skin gently abrades my sore nipples, making me feel even more. When he fills me up, I feel complete, so womanly and perfect. My body needs his seed so bad, and I suck it all up, milking him in the best orgasm of my life.

When we open our eyes, Stag is still buried inside me. Little fireworks from my orgasm still erupt inside me, but the big burst has passed. My stomach is swollen, full of Stag's cum and his love.

"That's a lot of cum." I smile, gazing down at my belly under which we're joined.

"Keep it all in, babygirl. You're not to waste a single drop." Stag's tone is commanding. He rubs my stomach, and I can imagine him doing the same when I'm knocked up and carrying his baby. It's such a serene, calming thought. The need to have a family with him is so pronounced. Stag is the perfect Daddy, a capable provider and a mature, stable man who can take care of me. I've always wanted to be with someone like him, and now that he's inside me, I know why none of those boys ever did it for me. No one can make me come like my Daddy.

Stag pulls out minutes later when he goes limp inside me. As he collapses on the bed, I can hear both of us panting. His cum leaks down my thigh, but Stag puts his finger next to my skin, lapping up that excess fluid and pushing it back into my convulsing hole. "That's where Daddy's cum belongs. In your pussy." His possessive gesture makes me hot all over. I close my thighs around his hand, trapping them there.

"Mmm...it feels so good when you're touching my pussy." He teases my slit after depositing my cum inside, rubbing my clit to keep me happy. When my legs loosen, he pulls his hand out.

"Come here, Ruby," he says, pulling my naked body next to his and cuddling me close. I moan and sink into his warm embrace. His snout kisses my hair, my neck, my shoulders, murmuring sweet nothings. "How did your first milking session feel?" he asks, rubbing his cum and my juices all over my sore nipples to soothe them. Every time he touches me, I burn for him. "Are your tits better now?"

"Much better," I reply. "Though nothing compares to the feeling of having your cock inside me. That was...out of the world."

"You have no idea how long I've wanted to do that," He gruffly whispers, still giving my udders some TLC. "You're so tempting, babygirl."

"As are you, hot minotaur Daddy." I sass him. "I just want to lie here naked with you and not go to work." I lay my hand over his that covers my belly. Lying against his hard chest makes me feel so safe. Turning my head, I touch his long snout, kissing his wet nose.

"What do you want to do instead, babygirl?" his voice is gentle.

"You really wanna know?"

"I do."

"Promise you won't judge me?"

"Ruby, I'll support you in whatever you want to do. I just want you to be happy, baby."

His words melt my heart. I always knew Stag was hot and capable, but I never knew he could be so caring. Having him say those words means the world to me.

"My dream," I clear my throat. "It's to get married and have lots of kids." I don't say it's him I want to marry. I still don't know how he feels about me. "I've always wanted to be a mom and have a big family. I know it's not as grand as taking over the business, but I think I'd love to create a warm home filled with love. When I was away at college, I realized how hard mom worked to create that happy home for us. I felt so lonely without her warmth. That's when I knew I wanted to be like her."

"It's an admirable dream," Stag says, kissing my cheek. "I know you'd make a great mom."

"You think so?"

"You're a natural nurturer," he says. "I was reluctant when your father said we wanted you to join the business. I knew you'd do great, but I guess I always had an inkling that your passions lay elsewhere. Whenever your dad brought the business up, you tensed up."

"Wow, you noticed that?" I'm surprised at how astute Stag is.

"You're so soft and giving, Ruby. You bring out the protective instinct in me. I want to keep you safe and give you a space where you can feel at ease." His hand rubs my stomach and my fantasy grows bigger.

"I feel at ease with you." My heart is in my throat. My feelings for Stag have grown ever since he milked me. I want to be near him, around his solid, reliable presence.

"I'm glad to hear that." He kisses me and we stay in each other's arms for a long time.

4

STAG

THREE WEEKS LATER—

I hear a knock at the door and look up from my work. The clock on the wall tells me it's almost lunchtime, and I know what that means. With a dirty grin, I say, "Come in."

The door opens and an angel materializes before me. Ruby is dressed in a floral white midi dress that flares around her hips. The square neck shows off a little of her cleavage, bunching around her fat hucow tits. I lick my lips at the sight of her heavy mounds engorged with cream. It's time for her milking.

"Good afternoon, Stag," she walks in, closing the door behind her. When the lock clicks, my cock twitches with anticipation. "I finished going through last year's marketing plan, and had a few ideas."

"I'd love to hear them," I tell her, beckoning her in. Ruby's lush, juicy body tempts me as she walks in, her hips swaying and those massive milkers bouncing with every step. I want to bend her over my desk and bury my cock in her heat right now.

It's been two weeks since she first started lactating. After

I milked her in her apartment and came inside her, Ruby decided not to go to the doctor.

"I want to keep producing milk," she said. "It's...a novel experience and it makes me feel like a mommy." With a naughty gleam in those baby blues, she added, "And I love it when my minotaur Daddy milks me."

There was no way I could say no to it. I loved her new milky tits too, loved how good it felt to hold her and drink from those massive udders. "Babygirl, if you keep lactating, I'm going to become addicted to you. I'll be draining those mommy tits thrice a day, and coming inside you every chance I get.

That's exactly what had happened for the last two weeks. I'd been fucking and milking Ruby regularly, and I'd come inside her so many times I'd lost count. I had no idea whether Ruby was on birth control or not, but the thought of knocking her up was growing on me. Every time I suckled her breasts and bred her, I longed to see her stomach swell with my baby. I needed reasons to make her mine.

Ruby takes a seat cross my desk, placing her small hands on the table. Instantly, mine cover hers, and we intertwine our fingers, aching to be with each other again. She's like a drug and I'm addicted to her. I've been considering proposing to her too. Marriage has never been a priority for me before, but having Ruby as my wife would be the greatest joy. After our first milking, she moved in with me, realizing it'd be more convenient for us to live together if I was going to milk her thrice a day. She's brightened up my home, and every time she's not there, I feel her absence. I need to put a ring on her finger ASAP, and tell her that her dream is now my dream too.

I can sense Ruby's nervousness, her fingers trembling in mine as she tells me her marketing ideas. After we made love and she started directly working with me, she's been enjoying work a lot more. I see her smiling more often, getting excited when we bounce ideas off each other. Though I know her dream is to be a mom and have a family, I wonder if working together might be something she enjoys too.

"Talk to me, baby. I'm not going to judge you."

"So, I was wondering if we could have tours of the farm." She looks up, her blue eyes large and filled with a mix of excitement and trepidation. "You know, people these days like to see how their food is made. We could organize group tours and show people around the farm. It'd be a good additional source of income and help get our name out there when people post about it on their social media."

"That's a fantastic idea." I bring her hand up to my mouth and kiss it. Ruby is so bright and full of life. I watch her eyes twinkle when I approve of her. "Maybe you should work on a plan and we could try presenting it to your dad and the others."

She nods, but the mention of her dad makes her doubt herself. "What's the matter, baby?" I let go of her hand and stand up. "Are you nervous about doing your first presentation?"

"A bit but..." She turns to me, and I know she's worried about not meeting her dad's expectations. "It's about dad. I still don't know how I'm going to tell him I plan to quit." Her blonde eyebrows crease together. "I've been enjoying work of late and..."

"It's making you doubt your original plan." I finish for her.

"It's still my dream to be a mom and devote my life to my family," she says. "But working with you is so much fun. I'm going to miss these afternoon milking sessions so much."

"So will I," I admit. Ruby stands up, coming closer to me. She's so much smaller than me, but that only makes me want to protect her more. "Maybe you could continue working part-time."

"Part-time?" She turns the idea around in her head.

"That way, you can take a break when you have kids, and set your own schedule. You'd have time to take care of the home, to spend time with your family, and you would still get to work on a few fulfilling projects. There'll be no pressure to do anything. We can take things at your pace."

"That...sounds like a good idea. I can't believe I never thought of it. But...wouldn't it be unfair to the other employees? I mean, I only get to do this part-time because my dad owns the company."

"We work with a few consultants and part-timers who set their own hours," I tell her. "I could take care of that for you."

"I don't know...I need to think more about it."

"Take all the time you need. I'm here to support you, whatever you decide to do, Ruby."

"Thank you. Having you around has been such a blessing." I hear her voice shaking, and notice that her eyes are a little teary. Ruby moves to me, putting her hands around me in a hug. I embrace her, feeling her warm, soft body move next to mine. "You're so nice to me, Stag. You're the perfect Daddy. I don't know what I'd do without you. Having you around has been so reassuring. I was worried when I started working here, but you've made the experience so good."

"Anything for you, sweetheart." I kiss her hair, my heart filled with longing. Giving her relief makes me feel better. I always want to see her happy and stress-free, doing whatever she loves. "Daddy loves making you happy."

"You make me so happy, Stag. I feel at home whenever

I'm with you. It's so reassuring to have someone who is always on my side. It's no wonder I've had a crush on you for so long. Maybe my heart already knew you were what I needed."

As she says those words, I feel a deep emotion move over my heart. It is then that I realize I'm in love with her. I am in love with Ruby.

The realization comes with a mix of elation and worry. She's much younger than me, and even though we've been having sex for weeks, I have no idea how John will react to us being together. Besides, I'm a minotaur and she's a human, and if we decide to get married, she might have to live on the ranch. I gaze down at Ruby, her beautiful face hitting me like a boulder. I want her in a white veil and dress, saying yes, when I gaze down at her next and kiss her.

My mouth closes over hers before I can think, and she submits to my kiss. Her eyes close and I lick and suckle on her juicy lips, tasting her desire. My hands slide down her back, cupping her ass and pulling her against my hard bulge. She grinds her pussy on my dick, telling me she's ready to be milked. I lift her up by the ass and she puts her legs around my waist, clinging to me as I carry her to the large couch in my office and sit down with her moving on my lap.

When our mouths part, she's panting, her skirt bunched around her ass. I tug at her floral dress and pull it over her head, leaving her in nothing but a pair of lacy white panties and a nursing bra.

"It's time for your milking, babygirl." I roughly whisper against her ear, licking the shell while my hands undo her bra. It falls to the floor, leaving her massive milkers exposed. Instantly, I cup her milky mounds, feeling their softness in my palm. "Mmm....Daddy missed those beautiful hucow tits. Is it just me or do they keep getting bigger every week?" I gaze at her fat titties, her nipples big as saucers and dotted with milk, begging me to suck on them.

"It's because you love

drinking my milk," she says. "My body produces more milk to keep up with the demand." Her hands are pulling my belt away, caressing my bulge through the fabric of my trousers.

"Well then, the demand's gonna get higher because Daddy can't keep his hands off your milky momma body." I smooth my hands over her hips, noticing that her stomach has gotten a little rounder, thanks to all the delicious food I've been feeding her. She looks so beautiful like this, all naked and dripping milk for Daddy.

"You're going to mess up the office," she says, even as her hands reach under her massive udders and hold them up, her nipples tight and beaded, perfectly suckable and ready to feed Daddy's mouth.

"I could always clean it up later. Reliving by babygirl's ache comes first." I close my mouth around one tip and suckle sweet cream straight from the source. My fingers twist around Ruby's panties and pull them off, leaving her wet pussy naked and grinding on my erection. Ruby moans, adjusting her sex against my bulge as she drips onto my pants. I guzzle mouthfuls of sweet cream, enjoying how her squishy nipples leak for me. I lick her soft tips, increasing her arousal, until she's begging me to take my pants off. Giving her tit one hard suck, I plop her nipple out of my mouth to fulfill her request.

"Doing this in the office feels so forbidden," she says, pushing my pants off my hips. I move, helping her slide them down my thighs, letting my cock spring free. My brown, ruddy erection is swollen and hard for my babygirl, veins pulsing all over. Ruby licks her lips, her eyes turning into dark blue pools like the ocean. She rubs her massive tits over my chest like a bitch in heat, her nipples arousing me when their rubbery tips brush against my leathery skin. "I need your cock so bad, Daddy."

"Mmm...I love how horny you get when I milk you, babygirl." I adjust her on my lap like a doll, my cock brushing against her slick folds. With every teasing slide, I make her leak more milk from her swollen tips. He pussy lips and pink and engorged, opening like a flower over the tip of my dick. I cup her shaven mound, teasing her lips a little before pushing my cock into the opening of her sex.

Ruby cries out when my big dick stretches her, invading her body conspicuously. But her cries turn into tumbling moans of pleasure when I drive in deeper, filling her up in one stroke. Putting my mouth to her other breast, I suckle her cream, feeling her fleshy walls clench around me as her letdown hits. She grabs my horns, feeding her her sweet cream as she moans, "Daddy...yes...please don't stop...you feel so good inside me..."

I begin to move in her narrow channel, feeling every rub of my cock against her most intimate part. I bounce her on my lap, steadily draining her cream, alternating between her udders. Ruby's milkers bounce and slap my face as she grinds up and down my length. I fuck her on the couch, drilling deep inside her pussy until I can feel the opening of her womb ready to receive my seed.

"Daddy....yes..." She grips my horns harder, her nutty scent surrounding me as we fuck like animals. She makes me lose control, bringing out the wild beast in me. Someday, I want to take her on the ranch, coming together on the green pastures where no one can hear her cries. As I pound her pussy, Ruby's orgasm begins to blossom. I feel her lose control, her body trying to take over.

"Come for me, baby." My mouth kisses her chest. In our frantic fucking, her tits bounce, spraying milk everywhere. The couch bears creamy proof of our lovemaking, but I'm too engrossed in my babygirl to care.

Ruby shatters on my cock with scream, coming with my dick inside her. I can feel the moment her body spasms, feel her pleasure flow through me like a river. I come inside her too, my balls bursting and filling her up with a cream pie. There's so much cum, it's filling her stomach up. But I keep rocking my hips into her, needing to feel her around me, as I drain her milkers. Suckling her sweet cream while I'm buried inside her is the best feeling in the world.

"I love you, Daddy," she says, when her eyes open. We're naked on my office couch, my babygirl covered in cream. But those words hit me hard.

Ruby just said she loves me.

She loves me.

My heart thuds in my chest, my cock pulsing in her channel. I just filled her up with my cum, and I have no idea if she's even on birth control. We've been doing this for weeks and...she could be pregnant.

But none of that matters. When I hear her sweet voice confess her deepest feelings, I know I feel the same way. She's been mine ever since she walked into this office.

"I love you too," I tell her, kissing her neck and jaw. "I love you. Ruby."

"What?" Her eyes widen, gazing at me. When she sees the seriousness in my eyes, her pussy quivers. "You...do?"

"Of course, I do, babygirl. You've put a spell on me. Having you in my house made me realize how lonely I was." My hands travel down her spine and squeeze her ass.

"You've turned my life upside-down with those milky tits, that tempting smile, and your dreams. I want to make your dreams come true, Ruby. I wanna give you the family you've dreamed of."

"Stag..." Tears fill Ruby's eyes.

I never thought I'd propose to my future wife in my office while we were still naked, and I was buried inside her, but this is the right moment.

"Marry me, Ruby. Stay with me here on this ranch. Let me make your dreams come true, babygirl. I know I'm too old for you, but you're the one I love. There's no other woman I want to share my life with."

"Stag...oh my god..." Ruby lowers her head, burrowing into my chest. I can feel her wet, salty tears run down my skin as she takes a moment. "You...really mean that?"

"I mean every word," I tell her. "Let me take care of you, sweetie. Let me be your Daddy for life. Let me give you babies and a home to nurture with your love."

Ruby's chest rises and falls with uneven breaths, and for a second, I'm worried she's not ready to get married yet. But when she meets my eyes, a soft smile curves her lips.

"I'm not sure about whether I want to work part-time or not, but I'm sure about this," she says. "Yes, Stag. Yes, I want to marry you. Oh my god, I still can't believe you asked me, but there's no other man I want to create a family with, no other man I want to love and cherish all my life. Let me be your safe space, Daddy. Let me be the home you come back to after a hard day of work."

There's nothing but love between us as I kiss Ruby, sealing our promise.

5

RUBY

TWO WEEKS LATER—

The bright sunshine looks even more beautiful as I open my eyes on Stag's bed. His side is empty, because he left for work earlier this morning, kissing me while I was still pretending to sleep. After he left, I rolled around, smelling him on the sheets and nesting in his side of the bed.

It's been two weeks since he proposed to me. We drove to the city and picked out a ring together. And then, he milked me and made love to me in the car on the way back.

My life's been filled with hot sex and endless bliss for the last two weeks. I raise my hand, watching his diamond glint on my finger and there's nowhere else I'd rather be. I know things are progressing fast, but I know Stag is the one for me with every beat of my heart. My hot minotaur Daddy has claimed me and he's the one I want to love for the rest of my life.

After Stag told me to make a marketing proposal, I managed to do some research and prepare a presentation on the guided tours. When I showed it to my colleagues at the ranch, they were thrilled, saying it'd be nice to have city folks visit once in a while, adding to the popularity of the town. Stag held my hand under the desk when we presented it do dad over video call, and I've never seen him prouder. Though I assume Stag called him up in advance and told him to be nice. After that episode, I've been seriously considering Stag's proposal to work part-time. Maybe I'm better at this than I thought I'd be, and working with my husband will give us more time together, and more common interests to talk about.

We still haven't told dad about our engagement yet, and my stomach feels a little sick. Stag called him up yesterday and asked him and mom to come over. They're coming today evening, and I have no idea how my parents are going to react to this engagement. I mean, Stag is as old as Dad, and though I'm all for the age difference, my parents might not feel the same way. Dad's known Stag all his life, but he can be incredible protective of me. As I sit up, my stomach gets worse. Nausea sweeps over me in a wave, and before I know it, I'm running to the bathroom, vomiting my guts out. I feel sick as I throw up on an empty stomach, my body feeling weak and tired.

I never thought telling my parents about my fiancé would make me so anxious.

I gargle my mouth and brush, going through my morning routine with a sense of dread. That's when my eyes hit the calendar, and I realize that I haven't had my period in over five weeks. It was due my third week on the ranch, but then, Stag proposed to me and I forgot all about it.

As my mind recollects all the times Stag came inside me, and milked me, I realize that there's a very good chance I'm pregnant. I wasn't on birth control when I came to the ranch, and though I got on it later, I might already have conceived. I blink at the mirror, feeling a glimmer of hope.

What if I'm really pregnant?

I never planned for it to happen so soon, but becoming a mom has always been my dream. Having Stag's baby fills me with joy, and the fact that we could be starting our family so soon after our marriage is even better. I know he loves me, and I know he wants to have children with me. The only thing to do now is to get a pregnancy test. It looks like I'm going to have to drive to town today.

∼

I'M DRESSED in royal blue dress, clutching two positive pregnancy tests, waiting for my husband to get back home. After I tested myself and all my tests came out positive, I couldn't wait to give Stag the good news. I rub my still flat stomach, feeling warm with joy at the thought of becoming a mom. Moving here to this ranch has been such a good experience.

The doorbell rings and I get it instantly. Stag steps in, tired from a day of work. He's dressed in his signature black pant, his big body and horns looking extra sexy to my horny, pregnant self.

"Babygirl, you look stunning." He leans over, brushing his mouth against my lips. When he holds me, I feel so precious. I sink into his big arms, enjoying the embrace.

"So do you." My heartbeats echo on my chest.

"Are you nervous about meeting your parents?" he asks, walking hand-in-hand with me to the couch.

"Yeah," I admit. Even more so now that I'm pregnant. They don't even know I'm seeing Stag. I have no idea how they'll react to my pregnancy. Stag's hand smoothes over my ass and that's when he feels the two hard tests in my dress pocket.

"What's that?" he asks.

"I...I have something to tell you," I say to him, taking a step away. He looks worried, wondering why I'm suddenly so serious. I reach into my pocket and grab the tests, holding them up.

In one breath, I announce, "I'm pregnant."

"What?" The voice I hear isn't Stag's. There's a high-pitched feminine voice and a deeper male voice. Stag and I snap our heads to the door where my parents stand, staring at us.

Dad is wearing a suit, his gray-white hair slicked back, and mom stands next to him in a pink suit and pearls, her long blonde hair tied up in a bun. I'm glad to see them but I just realize what they heard.

"What the hell is going on here?" Dad steps forward just as Stag reaches forward and grabs the pregnancy test. His angry eyes are on Stag, and I'm worried he might punch him. "Ruby, what do you mean you're pregnant?"

"Dad," I quickly push my body in between my dad and my future husband. Stag's eyes come around my stomach, gently rubbing it.

"Is it true, baby? Are you really pregnant with our baby?" he asks, his eyes filled with hope. He's ignoring Dad because my news means everything to him.

I nod, smiling a little when I gaze into Stag's big, brown eyes. "I just found out this morning."

"You're pregnant with...Stag's baby?" Mom asks, confused.

This isn't how I wanted to tell my husband, but well, now we've got to tell my parents too.

"I am," I confirm, turning my eyes back to my parents. I put my hand over Stag's big paw, grabbing one of his fingers. "Stag and I...we're..."

"Engaged." He finishes for me. I raise my other hand, showing off the diamond ring on my finger.

"What!?" Mom and Dad splutter together. Clearly, they didn't see this one coming.

"Ruby, please explain what's going on. I sent you here to learn the ropes of the business, and you're telling me you're engaged to my business partner and pregnant with his child?" Dad glares at Stag, and I can feel the animosity in the air. "I mean, he's old enough to be your father. You've never shown any interest in getting married before."

"I'm in love with her," Stag announces. "I didn't think it'd happen, but...when I saw Ruby again, I knew my feelings for her had changed."

"It isn't Stag's fault," I say right away. "I...I've liked him for a while."

"A while?" mom asks, raising an eyebrow.

"Before I went to college. He was just always around and...I developed feelings for him. My time at the ranch just confirmed those feelings. Dad, Mom, I really love Stag. He's the one I want to spend my life with."

"This is shocking," Dad says. "I never expected..." He glares at Stag. "I trusted you to look after my daughter, not knock her up."

"I will look after her for life," Stag says. "I promise you, Ruby will be my priority. I'll give her everything she wants, and make sure she's never unhappy."

"Are you sure?" Mom asks me. "Ruby, you're quite young. It might be too early to start a family."

"I'm sure," I tell her, holding Stag's hand. "There's something else I wanted to tell you too." I look up at Dad and Stag squeezes my hand, reassuring me that he's here with me. "Dad, I know you want me to take over the business, but I...I don't want to do it."

Milked by my Dad's Minotaur Friend 49

"What?" Dad takes a step back, shocked by my sudden pronouncement. "But Ruby...you just did that presentation and..."

"This business is your dream, not mine," I echo, tapping into the courage inside myself. "I...all my life, I went along with what you wanted because I didn't have the courage to express my true desire. But not anymore. Stag has given me the space to be myself, and do the things I love to do."

"And what is that?" Mom asks, her eyes seeking.

"I want to be a mom," I tell them. "I want to get married, have my own family, and devote my life to building a warm, happy home, the way mom did. I don't want to be wrapped up in professional responsibilities all day. I know how much Stag & Smith means to you, but I don't think I'm worthy of taking over such a successful business. Being at home around my loved ones makes me the happiest."

"Ruby..." Dad's eyes blink. "I...I had no idea..."

"I never wanted to work on the business, Dad," I tell him. "I wanted to tell you before I came over to the ranch, but I couldn't. But the moment I arrived at the ranch, I knew this wasn't the life I'd imagined. Spending time with Stag at his home, and having someone who got me, made me realize how real my dream was. Though I've come to enjoy work more than I thought I would, I don't think my original dream has changed."

There's a long moment of silence. Mom and Dad take a while to process everything I've just said.

"Why don't you sit down?" Stag asks them, gesturing to the couch. Mom sits first and Dad follows, both of them shell-shocked. Stag gets them some water, sitting by my side while we all process the news together.

"So, you'll be quitting soon?" Dad asks, gazing at my

still-flat belly. "I mean, you're getting married and everything."

"You're okay with it?" I ask him.

"It's not what I envisioned for you," he admits. "But I've also been a horrible dad…I can't believe I didn't even know what you wanted for so long. And Stag…" He blinks. "You're the most reliable man I know, but the thought of Ruby marrying you is still…a lot to take in."

"You'll get used to it," Stag says, holding my hand. "I don't know what I can say to reassure you, but Ruby is my whole world." He gazes lovingly into my eyes and I feel my heart ache for my minotaur Daddy. Fate has brought me to this perfect man, and now, we're going to have a family together. "She'll be safe and protected with me. I treasure her for life. Ruby's comfort is my priority."

"Well, I can't imagine any man who'd be better for Ruby," Mom says. Dad turns to her, his eyes wide. "Yeah, it's a lot to take in, but we've known him for years, John. Stag isn't like those immature young men who don't know how to treat their women. He'll be a good husband and father, and a steady presence is what Ruby needs."

"Thank you, Charlotte." Stag smiles at my mother. "I won't let you down."

"Ruby is precious to us," Mom says. "She's got an independent mind and once she decides to do something, she does it well. So, if she's decided to be a mom and a wife, I'm sure she'll excel at it."

I love the confidence Mom shows in me. My eyes move to her, filled with emotion. "I won't let you down," I tell them. "I know this news might sound sudden, but Stag proposed to me a while ago. We were just waiting for the perfect moment to tell you. And then, I found out about my pregnancy this morning...I guess that's two good news at once."

"I, for one, am excited about my first grandchild," Mom says. "It's been a while since we had a kid at home, hasn't it?"

At the thought of a grandchild, Dad perks up too. "Well, it was going to happen sooner or later." He turns to his business partner, finally giving in. "So, are you going to have minotaur babies?"

"I'm pretty sure we are," Stag says.

"We've got to get you married before Ruby begins to show," mom interjects. "How about a ranch wedding?"

"That sounds perfect." Stag and I smile together.

6

STAG

SIX MONTHS LATER—

Bright sunshine streams down on the wide expanse of green grass on the ranch. I walk hand-in-hand with my wife, keeping my steps slow to accommodate her. Bright light slides over her loose blonde hair, skimming over her swollen stomach. Over seven months pregnant with our first child, Ruby waddles by my side, making her heart flutter with every step. She's so beautiful when she's pregnant, her fat, milky breasts bouncing, and that big Mommy stomach making me want to take her right on the grass.

"Are we there yet?" I ask, wondering where she's taking me. This morning, Ruby said she had something to show me.

After we told her parents about our engagement and pregnancy, we ended up getting married within a month. As my beautiful bride said 'I do', right here on this ranch I'd built from scratch, I felt a deep sense of love like never before. For the last thirty years, I've devoted my life to cultivating this land and building Stag & Smith Dairy into what it is today. For the rest of my life, I'm going to be devoted to

Ruby, taking care of her needs day and night. We have a date night every week, and I make love to her every day, loving the way her body changes as she progresses through the pregnancy. After she became pregnant, she stopped lactating, but I know she's going to be a creamy mama after giving birth.

Ruby finished working on the project to bring in tourists to the farm, and we did a trial run of the idea last month. So far, it's been a huge hit. We're planning phase two of the project with more guests later this year. John approved it, and everyone's really excited about it. After submitting the final documents, Ruby went on maternity leave. She'll be taking a break from work to focus on our baby, but she said she'll consider working part-time once the baby's settled in.

"Just a little more," my wife says, walking me past some trees at the edge of the farm. The spot she's taking me to is behind our house, bordering the edge of the property. No one really comes here, and I wonder why she wants us to have a picnic date here. "I found this really secluded spot next to the trees last time I was out exploring the farms. I thought it'd make a nice date spot."

Ruby looks gorgeous in a red off-shoulder dress that flows over her big mama belly. Every time I look at her like this, I feel proud to be the father of her child. I love how well I've bred my babygirl, and how beautiful she looks as a pregnant mama. I can't stop myself from buying stuff for her, and thanks to my obsession with her pregnant body, she's got way more clothes than she could ever wear. We also finished making a nursery at our home two months ago, and have been buying stuff to welcome our son.

"Here," she says, coming to a stop at a patch of green grass that's surrounded by trees. It's nice and shady. "This is the spot I was talking about."

Ruby tries to bend, but I hold her hand. "Let me do it."

I spread the picnic blanket and put the basket on the ground. Then, I help her down. I wanted to have today's date at home, but Ruby insisted that she needed sunshine.

"I love it on the ranch," she said. "I'm so excited our kids are going to grow up here."

As Ruby sits down on the grass, I can't help but stare at my beautiful wife. I take a spot behind her, spreading my legs around her high so that she can feel my erection digging into her ass. My hands wrap around her big, seeded belly, gently caressing her baby bump. It feels so good to hold my pregnant wife, knowing she's going to pop soon.

"Babygirl, have I told you how gorgeous you look when you're pregnant?" I whisper against her ear, kissing her cheek.

"Only a million times," she says with a laugh.

Ruby has been reading up on parenthood and we've been attending classes for new parents at the local hospital, which happens to be an hour away. Still, I never miss an appointment to see how well our son is growing inside his momma's stomach.

"I'm hard all the time because of that hot mommy body. I want to keep you pregnant forever." I whisper as she puts her hands on my thick thighs.

"Well, we did say we wanted a big family," she teases. "And being bred by my minotaur husband is the best feeling in the world."

Her eyes are dark with lust when she turns to me. "Do you know why I chose this spot for our date, Daddy?" she asks, winking at me. I can see her fingers at work, pulling up her dress to reveal her creamy thighs inch by inch. When she gets to her belly, I inhale sharply, noticing that she isn't wearing any underwear. Opening her legs wider, Ruby flashes her bare pussy at me, hypnotizing me with those tender, pink folds that are coated with slick. "It's the best place to make love on the ranch. Nobody can see us here, but I get to be fucked by my hot minotaur husband on the grass."

"My god, baby. I love your filthy mind." My voice is raw need as I place my wife on the mat, climbing over her pregnant body. I pull her dress over her head and the sight of sunshine illuminating her naked body takes my breath away. Her breasts have gotten bigger, her juicy, pink nipples beading under my gaze. Her belly is round and swollen, ready to pop anytime.

"Babygirl, you're the most beautiful sight in the world." Her face is radiant with that pregnancy glow and her bright blue eyes gaze at me with pure lust. She's the most beautiful sight in the world, spread out on the blanket like a feast. I lean over, pressing kisses on her pregnant stomach. "Daddy loves looking at your radiant face and making love to this hot momma body." I run my hands all over her bump, caressing every inch of it. "I want to eat this hot mama for breakfast."

She giggles as my mouth moves down her belly, kissing her and loving her new, wider hips. My mouth settles over her mound, pressing little kisses onto the surface to make her hot. When she opens her legs automatically, I inhale the musky scent of her aroused sex, making me want to taste her pussy.

"Mmmm...Look at this slutty little pussy, already so wet for Daddy." I kiss her swollen folds before pushing out my big, cow tongue and swiping it all over her slit.

"Ohhh..." Ruby shudders under me, her body responding to my licking.

"Daddy loves playing with this ripe little pussy," I say,

finding her little pearl. My mouth is long, so it's a weird fit, but once I grab her clit between my lips, there's no letting go. I suckle my babygirl's sensitive bundle of nerves like a little juicy cherry.

"Stag..." Ruby grabs my horns, riding my face with her open pussy. I lick and suck on her clit, arousing her with lashes of my tongue and pulling of my teeth. By the time I'm done tasting her little pearl, she's shaking all over, begging, "Daddy...I think I'm going to come..."

"Not so fast, darling. Daddy's still not been inside your cunt." Letting go of her clit, I find her dripping hole and push my thick tongue into it.

"Aaahhhh..." Her pregnant hips arch, and I hold her baby bump as my fat tongue invades her pussy, stretching her. She drips honey all over my tongue, coating me in her juices as her body shakes and heats up. "Daddy...your tongue's so thick...like a cock..." She grinds her pussy all over my mouth, aching for that release.

"Baby, Daddy loves pleasuring your pregnant body. You're so responsive." I move my tongue in and out of her fleshy channel, making her hotter with every thrust. My tongue squeezes inside her pussy and licks her inner walls. When I find her sweet spot and lick it, she cries out loud.

"I'm coming..." Ruby's voice is music to my ears. I tease her G-spot again, and she shatters on my tongue, drowning me in her intoxicating juices. Her inner walls clench and massage my tongue, even as I continue thrusting into her and tasting every corner of that perfect pussy that's seeded with my son. I love making her come on my tongue, love feeling how she responds to every lick from her Daddy. Her smell surrounds me, her pleasure clamping on my tongue.

When I raise my eyes, she cracks open her blue eyes, her

face flushed with pleasure. "No one can make me come like my minotaur Daddy," she says, caressing my head with her hands. There's tenderness in her gaze as she touches my head.

Her legs are open, her thighs softly nestling my head. I retract my tongue from her cunt, swallowing her sweet juices. Watching her lying naked under the sun is a treat. However, when I raise my eyes to her bared breasts, I notice something unusual. Ruby's eyes slide down to her breasts which look a little bigger than before. But that's not the only unusual thing. Two fat beads of milk line her teats, making me lick my lips in disbelief. "Is that...milk?"

I can't believe it. My cock swells in my pants, my throat dry and aching to taste my babygirl's sweet cream again. I've missed milking her for the last few months.

"Surprise," she says, flashing me a big smile. "It came in today. I was so excited to show you. I know how much you love my milk. Daddy." Ruby cups her fat milkers, gently kneading them to release more droplets of milk. As her juicy nipple grows wet, my desire to feast on those big, ripe titties blazes out of control.

"Babygirl," I rub her bit stomach, kissing my way up her body to where she presents her big breasts to me. "That's the best news ever. Daddy's missed milking his hucow wife."

My snout settles over her pillowy breasts, kissing those squishy teats. They're extra-sensitive thanks to the pregnancy, and my little licks make my wife spew more milk from her tips. I put my mouth to one little bead and swallow it whole, circling her puffy areola with my teeth. My wife writhes against me, and I hold her hips down, feeling her big stomach bob against my body. When I suck on her bobbies, she floods my mouth with thick, nutty cream. Her pussy contracts when her letdown hits, rubbing against my covered cock.

"Mmmm...Daddy...Nothing compares to the feeling of your minotaur mouth on my teats, milking me like a hucow."

With a hungry moan, I swallow mouthfuls of her precious liquid, enjoying the feeling of sucking on her rubbery teats. My hands replace her, squeezing her mommy milkers for more delicious cream. She caresses my head, holding me against her breasts and cooing loving words. She'd make the most perfect mommy ever, with her nourishing body, and her giving manner.

When I've finished draining one boob, I latch onto the other, ravenous for my babygirl's cream. This is what made us get together, and milking her will always be a special experience for me. As my stomach fills up with her titty milk, my cock grows harder and harder until it's hard enough to tear through my pants. With a hard suck that makes her cry out, I drink more of her milk, eager to fuck my little hucow wife. When I've almost drained her breast, I pop her nipple out with a wet sound.

"Get on your hands and knees, baby. Daddy needs that hot pussy clenching around his dick."

Ruby complies, getting on all fours, pushing her big ass up at me. I squeeze her ass cheeks which are bigger and jigglier thanks to her pregnancy and feel the need to sink between those perfect fleshy mounds.

When Ruby is ready for me, her pussy open and welcoming, I undo my pants. My angry erection bounces free, massive and throbbing, and ready to sink into the heat of my wife's pussy.

"Are you ready to take Daddy's big cock, babygirl?" I ask,

rubbing the leaking tip of my monstrous erection all over her sensitive folds.

"Yes, Daddy." Her voice is breathy with need.

I push my massive dick into her cunt, feeling my wife's pussy stretch around me. She cries out, gripping the blanket as I invade her. Her body welcomes me home. My groin blazes with fire as her pussy swallows my rod, taking me all the way in until I'm securely seated inside her cunt.

"Every time I feel you inside me, I remember how huge you are," Ruby says, her fat tits dangling under her, dripping milk onto the blanket. My hands cup her pregnant stomach, holding it securely as I let her adjust to my size. "I'm never getting tired of having you inside me."

"Damn, your pussy is my home, babygirl," I say, feeling how tightly she grips me. "Daddy loves how perfectly we fit."

And then, I start to move. My cock is hungry and hard, my balls aching with unspent release. I rock my hips into her, holding her hips and stomach as I destroy her pussy with one deep thrust after the other. My balls slap violently against her ass, feeling her fleshy inner walls contract around my dick. I can't stop drilling her like an animal, feeling every scrape of my cock inside her fertile pussy.

"Daddy...oh my god..." Her breathy moans fill the air as I ride my pregnant, hucow wife like a bull, giving her pleasure under the open skies. I love how she looks with her big stomach bouncing and those hucow tits jiggling as her minotaur Daddy fucks her helpless little pussy raw. My hands cup her breasts, playing with her nipples as she takes my thrusts like a good girl. I can feel her tense, feel her need to come. When I grind my cock against her sweet spot, she can't hold it in anymore.

With a loud scream, Ruby climaxes, her walls clamping

around my dick as pleasure drowns her. I feel her drip more milk onto my palms, and I massage it all over her tits and pregnant stomach, taking my pleasure until her tight cunt chokes me into an orgasm. With a guttural cry, I climax inside my babygirl's pussy, drenching her in thick, hot ropes of cum.

Ecstasy skewers through my core, making my body surrender to the primal heat of our mating. Joined with my pregnant wife under the skies, I feel like the beast I am meant to be, one with nature and my lover. The earth is solid under us as my cells soak up every bit of bliss from our passionate joining. I can't stop myself from giving my seed to her, from filling her to the brim with my cum. My hands play with her milky nipples as she groans under me, receiving my seed like a vessel.

"Daddy...I love it when you fill my pussy with your seed," my wife says, her ass pushing up to meet my thrusts. "It makes me feel like I'm yours."

"You are mine, darling. Forever and always. Daddy's going to cream that pussy for life," I empty my balls into her fertile womb, feeling her milk me for more. If she wasn't pregnant already, she'd be now. The thought of breeding her ripe cunt again is already making my cock twitch inside her channel. There's nothing more filthy and forbidden than coming inside my pregnant wife while she's big enough to pop. And the fact that we're doing it naked in the wild makes it even more sexy. This is surely gonna be a pregnancy to remember.

I empty my balls into my wife's cunt, filling her with a cream pie as my orgasm bleeds out of me. We stay inside each other, panting and sweaty, and loving every moment of our passionate coupling. Everything is intense with her, and I love how perfect Ruby is for me. With her, I can be my natural self, a gentle daddy-dom, provider, and protector who takes great pride in caring for his babygirl.

When I finally stop coming, I pull out of my wife, loving how she drips my cum from her ravaged hole.

I lay down on the blanket, sweaty and panting, opening my hands to my pregnant wife. "Come to Daddy, sweetheart."

Ruby lays down on my chest, my hands cupping her pregnant stomach as we watch clouds float over the clear blue skies.

"That was the most amazing sex ever, Daddy," she whispers, as I lay my elongated snout on her shoulder. Her face turns and her lips kiss the side of my mouth. "It gets better every time."

"Well, that's because we're so perfect together, honey." I rub her stomach lovingly. "You're the best wife Daddy could ask for. I'm so lucky to have you. Every time I look at you ready to be a mom, I feel so proud of you, babygirl. You've made my lonely life a bed of roses. I'm gonna love you for the rest of time, Ruby."

With Ruby in the house, I no longer feel lonely. She's brought so much joy to my life that I didn't know was possible. Seeing her face every day, waking up to her every morning, and holding her every night is what I look forward to. She's the missing puzzle piece that completes my life.

"I love you too, Stag," she says. "I'm so happy I came here. There's nobody in this world who understands me better than you, Daddy. You've given me the space to be my feminine, nurturing self, and I'm so blessed to have a husband who supports me in every way. Living on this ranch has made me so peaceful. I can't wait to spend the rest of my life with you, loving you, and making you feel as blessed as you make me feel. Who knew I'd find my perfect match in my dad's minotaur best friend?"

My wife gazes at me, emotion in her eyes, and places her hand over mine. We both know that we've created this miracle from our love.

"Oh, darling." My mouth covers my wife's, my heart full of love for her.

This is the beginning of our happily ever after.

ABOUT THE AUTHOR

Jade Swallow is an author of super steamy novels. She loves reading and writing filthy tales featuring all kinds of kinks. Follow her on Instagram @authorjadeswallow for news about upcoming books.

Sign up for my newsletter here to get updates about my upcoming releases: subscribepage.io/eiSMM1

ALSO BY JADE SWALLOW

Want to read more in this series? Check out these books in the Married and Pregnant Monster Shorts series:

The Sea God's Fertile Bride : An age gap tentacle monster erotica (Married and Pregnant Monster Shorts #1)

Beauty and the Orc: An age gap orc daddy monster romance (Married and Pregnant Monster Shorts #2)

The Dragon's Maid : Age gap fated mates dragon monster romance with pregnancy, knotting, and milking (Married ad Pregnant Monster Shorts #4)

Looking for paranormal and omegaverse erotica? Check out these books by me:

The Vampire's Milkmaid: A gothic fated mates billionaire vampire romance with breeding, milking, and pregnancy (Paranormal Mates #1)

Stranded on the Shifter's Mountain: A Fated Mates Werewolf Shifter Romance with Breeding and Pregnancy (Paranormal Mates #2)

A Hucow Nanny for the Alpha Daddies: An age gap reverse harem fated mates omegaverse novella with pregnancy and milking (Omegaverse Daddies #1)

Alpha Daddy's Omega: An age gap pregnancy knotting and pregnant short story with arranged marriage (Omegaverse Daddies #2)

Love Daddy kink, breeding, and milking? Check out these books:

Breeding the Babysitter: A forbidden age gap billionaire romance with pregnancy (Forbidden Daddies #1)

Mountain Daddy's Curvy Maid : A grumpy-sunshine age gap romance with pregnancy and lactation (Mountain Daddies #1)

Pregnant by the Mafia Boss : A forbidden age gap mafia romance with pregnancy (Mafia Daddies #1)

Claiming my Ex's Dad: A forbidden age gap erotica

Milked by my Best Friend's Mom : An age gap lesbian erotic novella

Short story bundles:

Summer Heat Series Bundle (Summer Heat #1-5)

Feeding Fantasies Box Set (Feeding Fantasies 1-5 + 2 bonus shorts)

Creamy and Pregnant Short Stories (Billionaires & Hucows #1-5)

Creamy Fantasies Box Set (Creamy Fantasies #1-5)

Love dark college romances with steam and plot? Check out this one:

Broken (Twisted Souls #1)

She's a serial killer on a mission, and he's her next target. But things get complicated when she begins falling for him...